Be the Best
BASEBALL

Play Like a Pro

By Dick Walker

Troll Associates

Library of Congress Cataloging-in-Publication Data

Walker, Dick, (date)
    Baseball, play like a pro / by Dick Walker.
        p.   cm.—(Be the best!)
    Summary: Examines the equipment, skills, and rules associated with
baseball.
    ISBN 0-8167-1927-6 (lib. bdg.)   ISBN 0-8167-1928-4 (pbk.)
    1. Baseball—Juvenile literature.   [1. Baseball.]   I. Title.
II. Series.
    GV867.5.W35   1990
    796.357 '2—dc20   89-27392

Copyright © 1990 by Troll Associates

Printed in the United States of America.

10   9   8   7   6   5   4   3   2

Be the Best

BASEBALL

Play Like a Pro

FOREWORD

by Mike Sheppard

To do well at any sport, you must first have fun. And baseball provides as much fun as any sport I know.

The more you learn about baseball, the more fun you'll have and the better player you'll become. You'll learn a lot from this book, *Baseball, Play Like a Pro.* It's sound in technique. That's why I'm placing it at the top of my list of books for teaching young people the game.

Someday, like a few of the young players who have gone through my baseball camps, you may be lucky enough to make it to the pros. But even if you don't, you'll still be able to enjoy playing. And this book will give you the start you need.

Never lose your hustle!

Mike Sheppard

Mike Sheppard has been the head baseball coach at Seton Hall University since 1972. In 1987, Mike won his 500th game as Seton Hall's head coach. His winning percentage is over 70 percent. Three times, he was named Big East Coach of the Year. Seventeen times, he has guided Seton Hall to post-season tournaments, including two College World Series. And 54 of his players went on to sign pro baseball contracts. Aside from coaching, Mike was a star baseball player for both Seton Hall Prep and Seton Hall University.

Contents

Baseball—
Yesterday and Today

"Play ball!" That cry excites millions of fans every year. Baseball is one of America's most beloved sports. But baseball is not loved only in America. The sport of baseball is played and loved in many countries throughout the world.

How did baseball begin? No one knows for sure. Some baseball buffs believe the game was invented in 1839 by Abner Doubleday at Cooperstown, New York. The Doubleday story is a baseball legend that is widely supported.

However, other baseball historians think the modern game descended from a long line of ancient batting games. Over five thousand years ago, the Egyptians under the Pharaohs had batting contests with clubs and balls. The ancient Greeks and Romans also played batting games.

Long before Columbus discovered America, the Navajo Indians played a batting game with four bases. After hitting a ball with a hockey-shaped stick, a Navajo batter ran from base to base trying to escape being caught by players in the field.

In Britain during the 1700s, a game very similar to baseball was played. The game was called "rounders." It is still played today. Wooden posts are used as bases. A batter hits the ball and tries to run "round" the bases. Players in the field try to "put out" the runner by hitting him or her with the ball.

Early Americans played rounders in the mid-1700s and called the game "old cat," "moving's up," "town ball," and sometimes "baseball."

Baseball was played by soldiers in George Washington's Revolutionary Army. After America won its independence, people continued to play the game. America grew and so did the game of baseball.

In 1845, an American named Alexander Joy Cartwright, Jr., helped make the early form of baseball more like the modern game. Cartwright wrote the first baseball rules.

He also organized the first formal baseball team, called the Knickerbockers. The Knickerbockers and a club called the New York Nine played the first organized baseball game on June 19, 1846, in Hoboken, New Jersey. The Knickerbockers lost, 23-1.

In 1858, the National Association of Baseball Players was established. The league was responsible for printing the first official rule book.

Baseball's popularity continued throughout the Civil War. After the war, America went baseball crazy. By the year 1867, there were 237 teams in the National Association of Baseball Players.

From then on, baseball grew by leaps and bounds. Rules and equipment were continually improved. Americans became more and more interested in baseball.

The first professional baseball league was formed in 1871. The National League that still plays today was formed in 1876. The modern American League began in 1901. American Legion baseball for youngsters started in 1925. And in 1939, Little League was formed.

Today, baseball is enjoyed by millions of people all over the world. This book will help you to enjoy baseball and play it well. You will learn all about how to hit, throw, run, and field. So let's "play ball!"

What You Need
To Play Baseball

Where can you play baseball? Baseball can be played almost anywhere there is a large open space. Some forms of baseball are played in back yards, vacant lots, and even streets closed to traffic. Of course, the best place to play baseball is in a park or at a ball field.

What else do you need for a baseball game? You need a small ball. Baseball can be played with a rubber ball, a tennis ball, or a whiffle ball. A regular baseball is a special hardball.

You also need a bat to play baseball. Store-bought bats are made of wood or aluminum.

Next, you need four bases. For neighborhood games, anything from scraps of cardboard to squares scratched in the dirt can be used as bases.

But most important of all, you need players. A baseball team usually has nine players on the field, although games can be played with either more or fewer players. In fact, it only takes two players to have a game. One player has the ball. He or she is the pitcher. The other has the bat. He or she is the batter.

Pitcher

Batter

To start a baseball game, arrange the bases in the shape of a diamond. This is why a baseball field is sometimes called a diamond. Make sure there is an equal distance between each base along the edge of the diamond.

One base is home base or home plate. It is located at the bottom of the diamond. That is where the ball is batted from. To the right of home base is first base. The next base after that is second base. The base to the left of second base is third base. Both first base on the right and third base on the left are exactly the same distance from home base.

The field of play is determined by imaginary straight lines starting at home and running down the outside edges of first and third bases out into the field. Inside those lines is fair territory. Outside those lines is foul territory.

The pitcher stands a distance from home base and throws the ball so it passes over home plate. The batter tries to hit the ball into fair territory.

When the ball is hit, the batter becomes a runner and runs to first base. The runner may attempt to advance to as many bases as he or she can. If the ball is hit far enough without being caught in the air, the runner can move from first to second to third and then to home. A run is scored every time a runner goes around the bases and reaches home safely. A runner is allowed to stop at any base and wait for the next hit to advance. The object of the game is to score as many runs as possible.

Players in the field attempt to put out runners. A batter can be put out by swinging at pitches and missing three times. If a hit ball is caught in the air by a fielder, the batter is out. A batter can also be put out by being tagged with the ball before reaching a base. If a fielder with the ball touches the base before a forced runner reaches it, that is also a put out. Runners who do not stay on base can be tagged out anytime during play.

After the team in the field gets three put outs, they are up. When both teams get three outs each, an inning is completed. How long it takes to complete each inning determines how long the game will be. After a set number of innings, the game is over.

REGULATION GAMES

A regulation baseball game is nine innings. High-school teams play seven innings. Little League teams play six innings.

In regulation games, an umpire calls "balls" and "strikes." Four pitched balls outside the strike zone result in a walk, or a free pass to first base. A walk is often as good as a hit. But batters should still try to get on base by hitting, not walking. A pitch in the strike zone is a strike even if the batter does not swing. The strike zone is the area over the plate from a batter's armpits to the top of his knees.

Baseball also has many other complicated rules that an umpire must know in order to officiate a game correctly. Being an umpire is a hard job.

BASEBALL DIAMOND

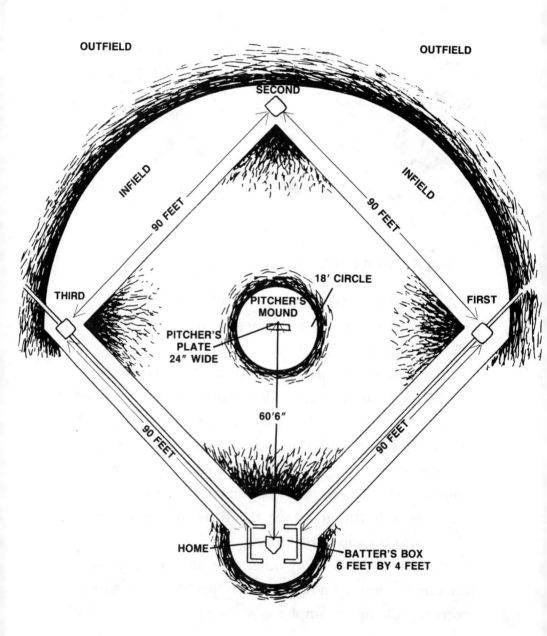

OUTFIELD

OUTFIELD

SECOND

INFIELD

INFIELD

90 FEET

90 FEET

18' CIRCLE

THIRD

PITCHER'S
MOUND

FIRST

PITCHER'S
PLATE
24" WIDE

60'6"

90 FEET

90 FEET

HOME

BATTER'S BOX
6 FEET BY 4 FEET

THE FIELD

A regulation field consists of an infield and an out-field. The infield is the area in front and just behind the bases. The outfield is made up of the far parts of the field beyond the infield.

The distance from base to base on a baseball field is ninety feet. (In Little League, the distance is sixty feet.) In the center of the diamond formed by the bases is a raised area called the pitcher's mound. It is sixty feet six inches from home plate.

The outfield dimensions of a field vary.

BASES

Baseball bases are stuffed rectangular pads or cushions that measure fifteen inches square.

HOME

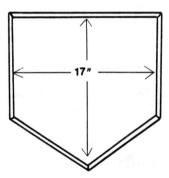

HOME BASE

Home base is a special thick-rubber plate seventeen inches wide and seventeen inches from the front to the back corner. It has five sides and looks like a rectangle with a triangle attached to one long side (the pointed part faces the catcher).

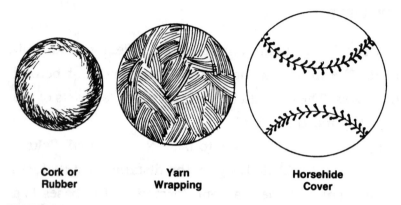

Cork or   Yarn   Horsehide
Rubber   Wrapping   Cover

THE BALL

A baseball has a center of cork or hard rubber. Yarn is wrapped around the center. The outside is made of white horsehide stitched together with thick thread.

A baseball weighs between five and five and a quarter ounces. It cannot be less than nine inches or more than nine and one-fourth inches around.

BATS

Years ago, all bats were made of wood. Today, aluminum bats are allowed in most baseball leagues except the professional ones.

Bats must be smooth and rounded. They come in a variety of weights and lengths. At its thickest part,

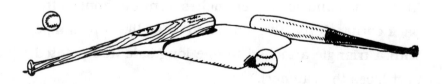

a bat cannot measure more than two and three-fourths inches. Nor can a bat be more than forty-two inches long.

Always take care of your bat. Don't leave it outside, and don't hit rocks or pebbles with it.

GLOVES

Baseball players wear gloves made of leather with webbing between the thumb and index finger. The webbing is called a pocket.

New gloves need to be oiled. Special glove oil can be bought. Oiling a glove makes the leather soft and easy to use. It also preserves the leather.

BASEBALL GLOVE

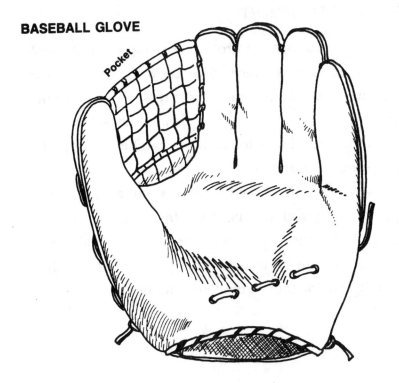

Pocket

CATCHER'S EQUIPMENT

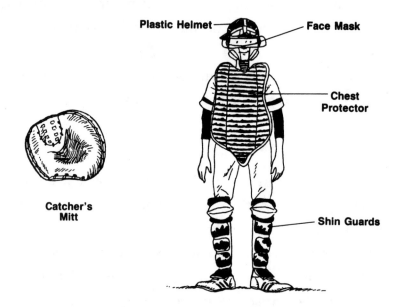

Plastic Helmet — — Face Mask

— Chest
Protector

Catcher's
Mitt

— Shin Guards

CATCHER'S EQUIPMENT

Catchers wear special protective equipment. A mask protects the catcher's face while allowing him or her to see clearly. The catcher's legs are protected by light but tough plastic shin guards. The padded chest protector protects the catcher's torso. Most catchers today also wear plastic helmets on their heads.

Boys who catch should always wear a plastic cup supporter to guard against groin injuries.

A catcher's mitt is specially shaped and stuffed with extra padding to take the hard throws of the pitcher. (See page 51 for more about the catcher.)

How to Develop Baseball Skills

What does a baseball player look like? That question has no answer. Good baseball players come in all shapes and sizes. Some are expert fielders. Others are great pitchers. There are power hitters and line-drive hitters. There are players who run bases well. A baseball team is made up of many different kinds of players.

THROWING

Throwing the ball is an important part of baseball. Fielders must be able to throw out runners.

In order to throw well, use the correct grip. The ball should be held between your first two fingers and your thumb. The rest of your fingers provide support. Spread your top two fingers a short way across the laces of the ball. Always use the same grip every time you throw.

BASEBALL GRIPS

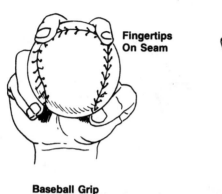

Fingertips On Seam

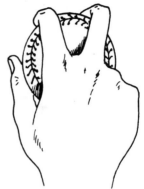

**Baseball Grip
Front View**

**Baseball Grip
Top View**

There are three kinds of throws. One is the sidearm throw. It is used for short, quick throws. The problem with this throw is that it is not always accurate. Also, it may put extra strain on your elbow and shoulder. If either begins to hurt, stop and rest immediately. Then try to develop an overhand or three-quarter throw.

The best throw for beginners is the overhand throw. An overhand throw is powerful and accurate. The ball is delivered by reaching way back behind the head and throwing in a smooth forward motion.

THROWING

A. Sidearm Throw   **B. ¾ Throw**   **C. Overhand Throw**

A variation of the overhand throw is the three-quarter throw. It is halfway between sidearm and overhand. This is a natural, very popular throw for many young players.

Before you throw, your weight should be on your back foot. Step as you throw, shifting your weight forward. That is called getting your body into the throw. It adds power to your throw. When throwing, always concentrate on a target. Don't throw aimlessly. Look at the person you are throwing to. As your arm comes forward, snap your wrist. That gives your throw a final burst of power.

As the ball leaves your hand, let it roll off your fingertips to give the ball spin. Then, follow through by allowing the motion of your arm to continue forward.

WARMING UP

Many players warm up before a game by throwing and catching a baseball with another player. Never try to throw hard or far at the beginning of a catch. Start close to your partner. Then spread farther apart as your arm loosens up. Throw softly in the beginning and then gradually increase the speed to your normal throwing level.

If you don't loosen up, you may injure or damage your arm. When warming up, try to throw to your partner's glove side. And always try to keep your throws between waist and shoulder level.

CATCHING

Concentration is the key to catching a baseball. Watch the ball as it approaches your glove. Do not take your eyes off the ball.

Always try to get in front of the ball instead of reaching for it from the side. For catching an above-waist baseball, have your glove slightly away from your body, with the palm out to the ball and the fingers pointing up. For catching a below-waist baseball, position your glove with the palm out to the ball and the fingers pointing down.

Try to catch the ball as you would a raw egg—softly. And try to catch the ball in the pocket of your glove. Look the ball all the way into the glove. Beginners should use *two* hands for catching. The free hand should be positioned behind the glove. Once the ball is in the glove, the free hand helps close the mitt to trap the ball.

Most important of all, do not be afraid of the ball. Do not close your eyes or jump to the side. Be confident.

Hitting

CHOICE OF BAT

Which bat should you use? Only you can make that choice. Select a bat that you can handle or control easily. It should not feel too long or too heavy. It should have a comfortable feel as you swing. Hold the bat out level with one hand and at arm's length. If you can do this for a few seconds, the bat you chose is probably right for you.

END GRIP

If you are a right-handed batter, your left hand should be nearest the nub or end of the bat. Your right hand goes on top of your left hand. (Reverse the position of your hands if you are left-handed.) There should not be any space between your hands. Grip the bat with your fingers, not your palms. Grip it firmly but don't squeeze it too tightly. Curl your fingers around the bat, wrapping your thumbs around your index fingers. Holding the bat at the very bottom is called an end grip. It gets the full weight of the bat into a swing and is a power hitter's grip.

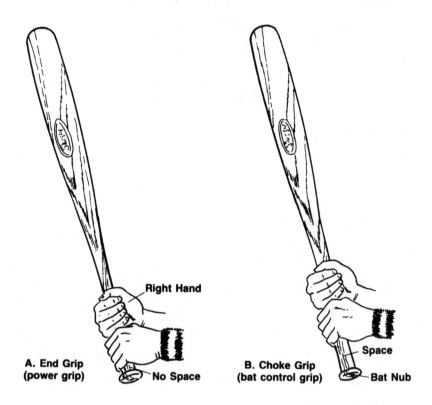

A. End Grip
(power grip)

Right Hand

No Space

B. Choke Grip
(bat control grip)

Space

Bat Nub

CHOKE GRIP

Some hitters "choke up" on the bat. The hands are positioned the same as in an end grip, but their placement on the bat is different. The hands are higher up the bat toward its thicker part. A choke grip gives a batter better control of the bat.

BATTING STANCE

In the batter's box, stand just far enough from the plate so you can touch the tip of your bat to the far side of the plate. When you swing, you will then be able to reach balls pitched over any part of the strike zone.

There are three basic batting stances you can try: parallel or even, open, and closed.

Parallel or Even Stance In this batting stance, both your feet should be placed the same distance from the plate. But the toes of your front foot can point slightly toward the field. This is generally not a very popular stance.

Open Stance Your front foot should be farther from the plate than your back foot in this batting stance. The toes of your back foot should point at the plate, and the toes of your front foot should point toward the playing field.

An open stance will give you a better view of the pitcher. It will also make hitting inside pitches (pitches close to your body) easier. But it makes hitting outside pitches much harder. That's because your bat swing in this stance will tend to pull you away from the plate. When that happens, you are "stepping in the bucket."

Closed Stance When your front foot is closer to home plate than your back foot, you're in a closed batting stance. This will allow you to hit both inside and outside pitches. It is a good stance for beginners to use.

BATTING STANCES

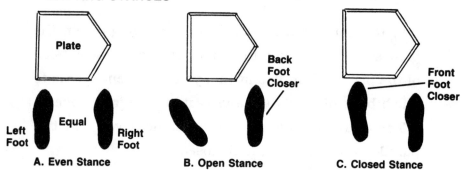

A. Even Stance B. Open Stance C. Closed Stance

Be comfortable in your stance. Stand with your weight balanced. Keep your knees and hips relaxed. Your arms should be away from your body, with the bat held chest high or higher. Do not hold your bat too low or keep your arms against your body. And never hit with the bat resting on your shoulder.

Keep your shoulders level. Turn your head toward the pitcher and watch the ball in his hand. Some batters like to crouch or bend their knees a bit. Do what feels comfortable for you. It sometimes helps beginning batters to keep their back elbow horizontal. That makes for a more level swing.

STRIKE ZONE

Good hitters are smart hitters. They swing only at pitches in the strike zone. That is called having a "good eye." The strike zone is the area over the plate from the top of a batter's knees to just below the shoulders. This differs for each batter. Learn your strike zone. Get yourself into the habit of not swinging at bad pitches. Pitches in the strike zone are the best ones to hit.

TIMING AND SWINGING

Timing is swinging at the right moment and hitting the ball at the right spot. Where the ball goes when you hit it is an indication of your timing.

A right-handed batter who hits to right field is more often than not *swinging late*. The bat is hitting the ball after it passes the batter during the beginning of the swing.

A right-handed batter who hits to left field is usually hitting *out in front* or *pulling the ball*. The ball is hit before it reaches the batter during the end of his or her swing.

A ball hit up the middle of the field is perfectly timed. It is hit in the middle of the swing. But not every hit has to be perfectly timed. Different pitches are hit and timed different ways. Good timing means making solid contact with the ball.

As the pitcher prepares to throw, concentrate on the ball. The batter's weight should be shifted to the rear foot. As the ball approaches, take a short stride forward with the front foot. Always step into the pitch.

The hips rotate forward as the swing starts, leading your hands through the swing. The shoulders remain level. If you dip your front shoulder, you will hit ground balls. If you raise your front shoulder, you will hit fly balls. Watch the ball all the way in. Keep the bat level, extending your arms out from your body as you swing. Your back leg bends at the knee while the front leg remains straight. Your weight now shifts forward.

Good Stance

Weight Back

1.

Hips Rotate

Weight Shifts

Step

2.

Shoulders Level

Eye On Ball

3.

Wrist Action

Extend Arms

Hands Roll Over

Follow Through

Straight Leg

Bent Leg

4.

If your timing is good, your hands will be in front of your body before the bat is squared around to meet the ball. Try to watch the ball hit the bat. Grip it more firmly at impact. Do not turn your head away as you swing.

As you swing, use your wrists to whip, or snap, the bat when you make contact. Most home-run hitters have great wrist action. Don't stop your swing. Let it continue. This is a batter's follow-through.

And remember, never throw the bat. Just let the bat drop to the ground as you begin to run.

THE SACRIFICE BUNT

The sacrifice bunt is used to advance a runner already on base (usually from first to second). The batter gives up the chance for a hit in order to move someone on base into a better position to score. A sacrifice bunt does not count as an official at-bat, so it never hurts a hitter's batting average.

Even though there's no chance for a hit, the batter must still rely on good hitting technique to sacrifice bunt effectively. First, the batter should assume a bunting stance. This is done by turning to face the mound *before* the pitcher delivers the ball. The batter's toes should be pointed at the pitcher. It is a simple one- or two-step operation. It is called "squaring around."

As the hitter turns, the bat is repositioned for a bunt. The top hand slides down the bat and grips the barrel between the fingertips *only*. If you keep your fingers curled around the bat, you may get hit with the ball. The bottom hand remains near the nub, with the fingers curled around the handle.

The bat is held out from the body at the top of the strike zone in a level position. The barrel part of the bat should extend out over the plate. The batter stands in a crouched position with head up, awaiting the pitch.

As the ball approaches, keep the bat level. Do not raise or lower the bat to meet the pitch. Raise or lower your entire body by bending at the knees.

Do not swing at the ball and do not lunge at it. *Let the ball hit the bat.* The ball should bounce off gently.

BUNTING POSITION

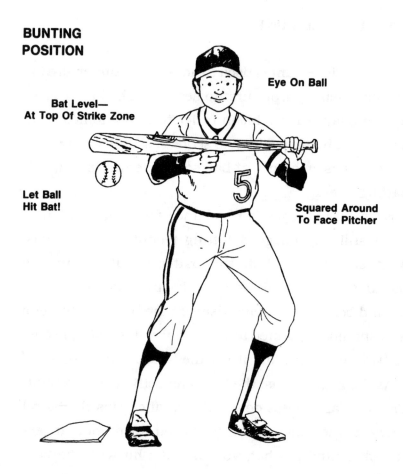

Eye On Ball

**Bat Level—
At Top Of Strike Zone**

**Let Ball
Hit Bat!**

**Squared Around
To Face Pitcher**

Try to position your bunt so it lands between the pitcher's mound and third base or between the mound and first base. You do not want to hit the ball straight back to the pitcher. It will be too easy for him or her to field it and throw out the runner at second. You also do not want to pop the ball up into the air where it can be easily caught. So keep the bat level and direct the position of the ball by moving the barrel of the bat forward or backward with your hand. The hand at the nub stays steady.

Fielding

Fielding is an important part of baseball. Infielders are often used more for their defensive ability than for their offensive ability.

Years ago there was no such thing as a defensive outfielder. Today there is. Watching a player execute a beautiful fielding play is just as exciting as watching a home run sail into the stands.

READY POSITION

To field well, a player must be able to get the ball. Standing in a baseball-ready position will help you get to the ball quicker.

Never stand straight up with your arms dangling at your sides. Spread your feet. Keeping your arms up, bend slightly at the knees and lean a bit forward at the waist. Put your hands *lightly* on your knees. Never rest by leaning too far over and putting all your weight on your hands.

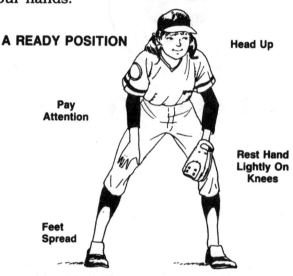

A READY POSITION

Head Up

Pay
Attention

Rest Hand
Lightly On
Knees

Feet
Spread

Stand with your weight a bit forward on the balls of your feet. You are now ready to move quickly in any direction. Be prepared before each pitch. Relax after the pitch.

PAY ATTENTION

While in the field, always pay attention. Know how many outs there are. *Do not daydream,* especially in the outfield. Watch the batter. Before each pitch, know where you should throw the ball if it is hit to you. That is called "being mentally in the game."

INFIELD PLAY OR FIELDING GROUND BALLS

Always try to field ground balls in the middle of your body. That means moving your body to a position in front of the approaching ball. In baseball that is called "getting in front of the ball."

To field a grounder, *do not* bend over at the waist. Bend at the knees, lowering your body toward the ground. Keep your feet spread for balance. The correct fielding position is a squatting position a little like a catcher's position.

WRONG WAY TO BEND FOR BALL

Wrong! Backside Up

Wrong! Bent At Waist

Wrong! Knees Locked

RIGHT WAY TO BEND

Low Squat Position

Backside Down

Head Down

Knees Bent

Fielding Out In Front

As you crouch to field a ball, your weight should be forward toward the front of your feet. Keep your eye on the ball. Field the ball out in front of your body by placing the edge of the glove, palm up, on the ground. Use both hands. This will prevent the ball from scooting past you under your glove.

As the ball comes into the glove, use your throwing hand to scoop the ball into the mitt and trap it there.

Fielding with two hands allows the player to come up throwing. The throwing hand is already on the ball and does not have to reach in to get the ball out. That saves valuable seconds in throwing out a speedy runner.

CHARGING THE BALL

A slowly hit ground ball should be charged. That means a fielder does not wait for the ball to come to him or her. The fielder moves to meet the ball.

Very slowly hit balls can sometimes be fielded with just the glove hand or with just the throwing hand. But it takes practice to master that charge, scoop, and throw.

CHARGING SLOWLY HIT BALL

Run Under Control

Stay Low

Eye On Ball

Glove Down

BALLS HIT TO THE SIDE

If a ground ball is hit sharply off to the side of a fielder, he or she will have no chance to get in front of it. In such a case, the fielder makes a deep angle toward the ball in an attempt to cross its path before it reaches the outfield.

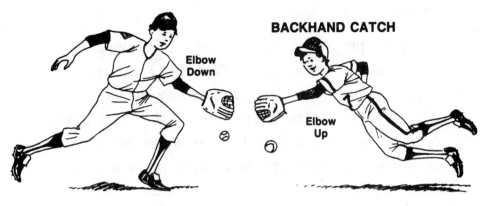

BACKHAND CATCH

Elbow
Down

Elbow
Up

FOREHAND CATCH

For a ball hit to the left of a right-handed fielder, the fielder stretches for the ball with his or her glove hand, elbow down. This is called a "forehand catch." For a ball hit to the right side, the stretch for the ball is with the glove hand, elbow up. That is called a "backhand catch." These types of catches are difficult even for excellent fielders.

THROWING TO A BASE

Infielders have a twofold job. First, they must catch the ball. Second, they must throw out the runner. Getting rid of the ball without delay is a must. That's why fielding with two hands is so important. Before you throw, always plant your back foot so you can throw off of it. Do not throw wildly without looking. Do not make a throw unless you have a chance to get a runner out. The best throws are chest high to the glove side of the player you're throwing to. They are easy to handle.

FIELDING FLY BALLS

Outfield play differs in many ways from infield play. In the outfield, most of the balls are hit in the air.

In the outfield, a fielder must be ready and pay attention at all times. More often than not, the ball *will not* be hit directly to the outfielder. He or she will have to go to the ball. Knowing which way to move and doing it quickly is called "getting a jump on the ball."

Once a fly ball is hit, the outfielder judges which way it is going (right or left). He or she then turns toward the ball by pivoting on both feet. An outfielder's first step is taken with the foot nearest the direction of the ball (hit to the right, step with the right foot). Getting a jump on the ball is part instinct and part practice.

CATCHING A FLY BALL

A good outfielder always hustles to get in position to catch a ball coming down. That is called "getting under the ball." Keep your eye on the ball. Raise your glove hand with the palm up (the back of your hand toward your face). Your throwing hand should be next to your glove. Always use two hands.

Position yourself so you are one step back. This is so you can step forward while making the catch as you prepare to throw.

Let the ball drop into your glove. Never lunge at the ball or wave at it. Never shut your eyes or turn your head. Try to catch the ball in the pocket. The catch

Eyes On Ball

Glove Out In Front

Two Hands Under Ball

Let Ball Drop In Glove

Step

1. Cover ball with hand after catch.

2. Get ball into infield quickly.

FIELDING FLY BALLS   **AFTER CATCH**

should be made just above eye level in the middle of the body, not off to one side. When the ball is in the glove, squeeze it and use your bare hand to cover it so the ball does not pop or drop out.

FIELDING GROUNDERS IN THE OUTFIELD

The surest way to field a grounder in the outfield is first to get in front of the ball. Then drop one knee to the ground and get your glove out in front between your legs. That way, if you mishandle or don't catch the ball, you will block it with your body and keep it in front of you. One of the most important outfield rules is never to let a ground ball get past you.

FIELDING GROUNDERS IN OUTFIELD

Knee Down

There are times when an outfielder must charge a ground ball and field it as an infielder does (see page 33). This happens when an outfielder must make a throw to a base on the following play.

THROWING FROM THE OUTFIELD

Outfielders should always use an overhand throw (see page 20). Unless an outfielder is very close to a base, the throw to a base should never be in the air. A throw from the outfield should always bounce once (and just once) before reaching a base. Also, outfielders should know ahead of time what they're going to do with the ball once they catch it.

On extremely long throws, outfielders should throw the ball to the *cutoff*. A cutoff is an infielder who goes partially into the outfield to help relay a long hit ball to a base. Always remember never to hold the ball in the outfield. Get rid of it quickly.

Base Running

Hustle is the key to good base running. Never loaf because you think a hit ball will result in an easy out. In baseball there are no easy outs!

BASE LINES

Base lines are imaginary lines formed by connecting the outside edges of the bases. A runner is automatically out if he or she runs more than three feet outside the base line to avoid being tagged.

RUNNING TO FIRST BASE

Getting out of the batter's box quickly is important to good base running. After swinging, a right-handed hitter takes his or her first step with the back or right foot.

The hitter's stride should be directly toward first base. The front or left foot is used to push off.

A left-handed batter's first step is with his or her left foot, which is the back foot. It is like a pivot step. The push-off is with the right foot.

When running to first base, always run *through* the base, making sure to touch it with your foot. Do not slow up before the base or try to come to a dead stop at the base. Continue to run hard until you are past the base. This is the fastest way to get to it.

RUNNING THROUGH FIRST BASE

Some beginners make the mistake of sliding into first base. Sliding into the base takes more time than running through the base. The *only* time a runner slides into first base is if a throw pulls the fielder off the base. The fielder will then try to tag the runner. *A runner slides into first base only to avoid a tag.*

EXTRA BASES

When taking extra bases on a hit, there are two important things to remember. The first is to start to turn before you reach the base. Do not run straight to first and then turn toward second. Start to turn toward second before you reach first. Always start every turn before reaching the base.

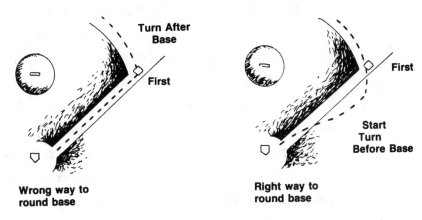

Wrong way to round base

Right way to round base

Where your foot touches the base is the next important part of running for extra bases. The correct way to run for extra bases is to touch the inside corner of the base. Stepping on the middle of the base will only slow you down.

FOOT TOUCHING BASE

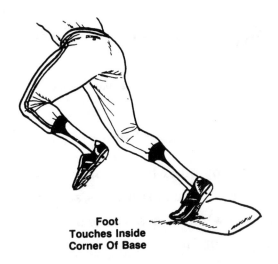

Foot
Touches Inside
Corner Of Base

GENERAL RULES

When running bases, beginners should always remember several general rules. A base runner cannot pass a runner in front of him or her. So watch the runner in front of you. Do not run on a fly ball. If you are on first or second base, go halfway to the next base when a fly ball is hit. If it is caught, return to your base. If it is dropped, advance to the next base.

With less than two out, a runner on third base should stand on it when a fly ball is hit. That is called "tagging up." If the fly ball is hit deep enough, the runner can tag up when the ball is caught and then run for home base.

RUNNER TAGGING UP

Foot On Base Until Catch

Third Base

There are many other base-running rules. Here is an important one: If a base runner is struck by a hit ball in fair territory while off base, he or she is automatically out. So watch out for hit balls!

Sliding

When there is a chance a runner will be tagged out at a base, the runner should slide. A mistake beginners often make is that they slide too late. They start a slide when they are too close to the base. A slide has to be started early, about three to four steps from the base.

STRAIGHT-IN OR BENT-LEG SLIDE

For the straight-in slide, approach the base with body erect and eyes on the base. Begin the slide with whichever leg is more comfortable for you. Say it is your right leg. As you approach the base and begin the slide, bend your right leg at the knee, folding it under you. Extend your left leg toward the base. Keep the heel of the extended foot up. Make sure the foot of the bent leg is turned sideways. (Otherwise, if you wear spikes, they might snag the ground.)

The upper torso leans back. Keep your arms up. That is important. Keeping them down can result in hand injuries.

Relax, and try to spread out the force of your slide over the entire length of your body. The extended leg makes contact with the nearest part of the base.

BENT-LEG SLIDE

HOOK OR FALL-AWAY SLIDE

The *hook slide* is a good slide to use to avoid a tag. It gets its name from the fact that one foot hooks a corner of the base.

The slide is started like a straight slide. But as the runner leans back to slide, both legs are bent feet out. The lead leg (depending on which side of the base you are sliding to) is then stretched out. The slide actually occurs on the thigh and rump of that leg.

HOOK SLIDE

The other leg remains bent (not under you) out to the side and slightly behind. You slide by the base, hooking it with the foot of your back leg. Remember to keep your arms up. A hook slide can be done to either side of the base.

Important Note: Sliding should *not* be practiced without the help of an adult instructor who knows the proper techniques. Among the places you can practice sliding are on a ball field, on a long, padded vinyl mat, or in a long sand pit.

The Pitcher

There are nine positions on a baseball team, and the position of the pitcher is one of the most challenging to learn. A pitcher has to have a strong arm and be smart. He or she studies batters and sets them up for pitches. A good pitcher needs at least two or three solid pitches. Usually those pitches are a fast ball, curve ball, and change-of-pace or off-speed pitch.

CONTROL

Control means a pitcher has the ability to throw the ball where he or she wants to most of the time.

There are ways to improve control. When playing catch, always throw to a target. Concentration also helps a pitcher's control. Look at the target the catcher is giving you and concentrate on throwing to it.

THROWING

Young pitchers must take special care to guard against hurting their arms. Warming up (see page 21) is crucial before actual pitching. A sufficient amount of rest (several days) is a must between pitching assignments. No matter how important the game is, a young pitcher should never pitch with a sore arm.

Most young pitchers can do well in beginners' leagues if they throw hard and have good control. So we will concentrate on throwing the hard pitch—the fast ball.

A pitcher should use the same grip every time he or she throws a fast ball. Most good fast-ball pitchers grip the ball with two fingers across the widest part of the seam. Another popular fast-ball grip is with two fingers across the narrowest part of the seam.

FAST BALL GRIPS

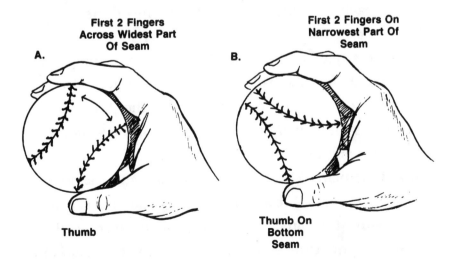

A. First 2 Fingers Across Widest Part Of Seam

Thumb

B. First 2 Fingers On Narrowest Part Of Seam

Thumb On Bottom Seam

WIND-UP

To pitch with no runners on base, a pitcher stands on the mound facing home. A right-handed pitcher puts his or her right foot on the pitcher's plate, or rubber. The left foot is behind it. (The reverse is true for a left-handed pitcher.) The weight is on the back foot. The ball is held behind the back to hide it from the batter's view.

Next, the pitcher begins a motion called a wind-up. The pitcher bends forward, shifting his or her weight to the front foot. As this happens, the arms swing backward and the knees bend slightly.

As the pitcher straightens up, the weight is shifted back to the rear foot. The arms swing forward. As the arms come forward, the hands join, putting the ball and glove together.

As the arms rise up over the head, the pitcher's eyes are on the target. During this part of the arm swing, the foot on the rubber turns out slightly. As the joined hands reach the final point above the head, there is a brief pause.

After that pause, the arms come down and the pitch is started. Before the ball is delivered, the pitcher leans slightly back to get his or her body into the throw. The back leg is lifted as it comes forward. All the weight is on the foot on the rubber (front foot). The back foot steps toward the plate. The pitcher pushes off with the other foot. The pitch is thrown in one fluid motion (see page 20). Lastly, the pitcher follows through, keeping the throwing arm at the side of the body and ending up in a balanced position facing home.

PITCHING WIND-UP

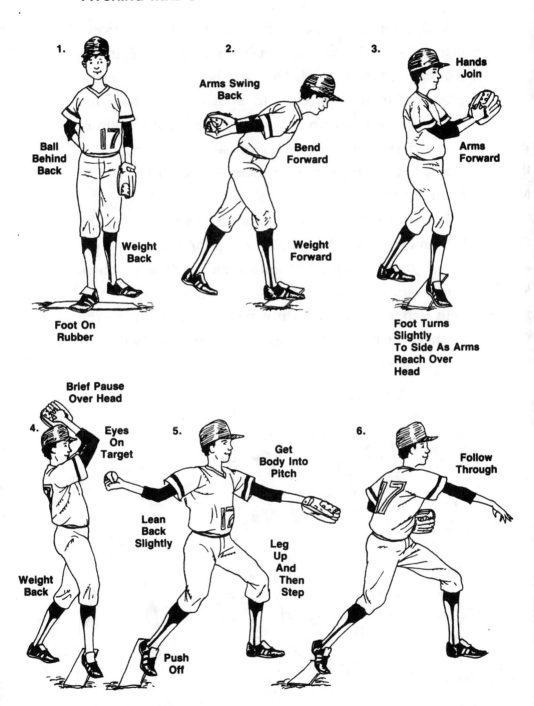

1.

Ball
Behind
Back

17

Weight
Back

Foot On
Rubber

2.

Arms Swing
Back

Bend
Forward

Weight
Forward

3.

Hands
Join

Arms
Forward

Foot Turns
Slightly
To Side As Arms
Reach Over
Head

4.

Brief Pause
Over Head

Eyes
On
Target

Weight
Back

5.

Lean
Back
Slightly

Push
Off

Get
Body Into
Pitch

Leg
Up
And
Then
Step

6.

Follow
Through

17

STRETCH

With men on base, a pitching *stretch* is used instead of a wind-up. The stretch starts with the pitcher standing sideways on the mound. The right foot of a right-handed pitcher should be directly in front of the rubber but always in contact with it. The left foot should be in front of the right foot, with both feet parallel to the rubber. (The reverse is true for left-handed pitchers.) The weight is on both feet.

The pitcher raises his or her arms upward, joining the ball and glove hands while lowering the arms. With the hands joined, the pitcher rests them near the middle of the chest for a second. After a pause, the pitch can be delivered to the plate or thrown to a base. However, the pitcher who throws to a base must step directly toward that base as he or she throws.

PITCHING STRETCH

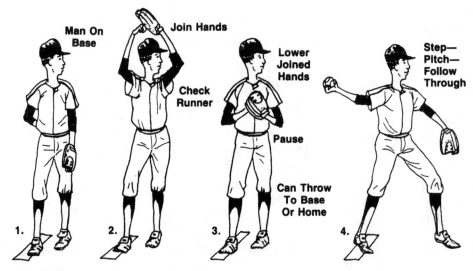

Man On Base

Join Hands

Check Runner

Lower Joined Hands

Pause

Can Throw To Base Or Home

Step— Pitch— Follow Through

1.   2.   3.   4.

Pitching Rubber

The Catcher

A catcher must have strong legs and a strong throwing arm. He or she is in charge of the infield and is a team leader. The catcher also must study the batters to help the pitcher set them up for pitches.

CATCHER'S CROUCH

To get in a catcher's position, first spread your feet. The left foot should be slightly in front of the right foot. Bend at the knees, lowering your body into a semi-crouched stance. (Never sit back on your heels or catch with one knee resting on the ground.) Stay balanced on the balls of your feet.

CATCHING

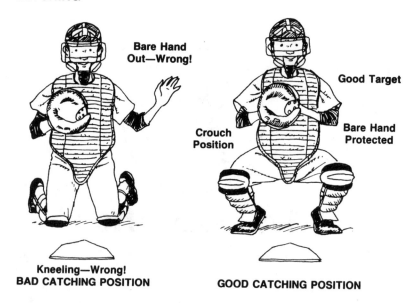

Bare Hand Out—Wrong!

Good Target

Crouch Position

Bare Hand Protected

Kneeling—Wrong!
BAD CATCHING POSITION

GOOD CATCHING POSITION

Hold up your catcher's mitt (see page 18). That is called "giving the pitcher a target." He or she will try to throw where you put your catcher's mitt. Once the target is up, do not shift it. However, do not keep the same target area for every pitch or every batter. Move it to different areas of the plate, depending on where you want the pitch thrown over the plate.

Always be in a ready, semicrouched position to receive the pitch. Between pitches, the catcher can rest by dropping to one or both knees. A catcher needs very strong legs.

POSITION OF BARE HAND

A catcher's bare hand is very vulnerable to injuries. When you catch a pitch, it must be protected. Today, most catchers put their bare hand behind their backs when catching a pitch. Another safe position for a catcher's bare hand is directly behind the mitt itself, palm forward. Never leave your bare hand unprotected in front of your body.

CATCHER'S THROW

Cock Arm
Above Back

Quick Snap
Overhand Throw

CATCHER'S THROW

A catcher's throw differs slightly from the throws described earlier (see pages 19-21). A catcher uses a short, snap throw because of its power and quick release. The throw is similar to an overhand throw. And the movement of the throw is overhand. The difference is the catcher cocks the ball above his or her back. The arm and hand move forward in a short, snapping overhand motion.

Other Baseball Positions

The other seven positions on a baseball team require different mental and physical skills.

FIRST BASE

First base is a natural place for left-handed infielders. First base is usually played by someone tall with long arms and legs. He or she often has to stretch out when there's a long infield throw or close play to get a runner out at first base.

SECOND BASE

To play second base, you need to be quick, agile, and a good fielder. You also must work well with the shortstop on double plays.

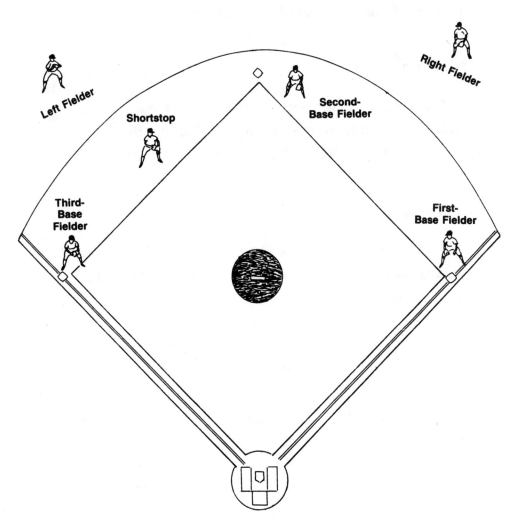

Center Fielder

Right Fielder

Left Fielder

Shortstop

Second-
Base Fielder

Third-
Base
Fielder

First-
Base Fielder

SHORTSTOP

The shortstop is also an excellent fielder. It takes a slightly stronger arm to play shortstop than second base.

THIRD BASE

To play third base, you must be able to handle line drives hit down the line. You must also have a strong arm for the long throw to first. In the pros, players who play third base are usually solid hitters too.

CENTER FIELD

The center fielder is the captain of the outfield and takes any ball he or she can reach. Usually, the center fielder is the fastest outfielder and the best fielder.

LEFT FIELD

The left fielder handles more ground balls and line drives than the other two outfielders. He or she is good at judging the ball.

RIGHT FIELD

The right fielder has the best throwing arm of any outfielder. The throw from right field to third base is the longest throw in baseball.

Hitting Drills

STRENGTHENING WRISTS

All good hitters have strong wrists. Doing pull-ups can help develop your wrists as well as your arms and shoulders. Pushups done on your fingertips also strengthen the hands and wrists. Remember to spread your fingers.

SWINGING THE BAT

Just swinging a bat is a good way to develop a level swing. Get into your stance, take a step, and swing, all the while concentrating on a level cut (see pages 25-28).

There are several other ways to work out with a bat alone. It is possible to draw baseballs in chalk on a wall at different levels in your strike zone. Look at the chalk balls. Step and swing as if they were pitches. Remember to stand clear of the wall so your bat does not hit it. After you're through, be sure to clean off the chalk marks on the wall.

CHALK DRAWINGS DRILL

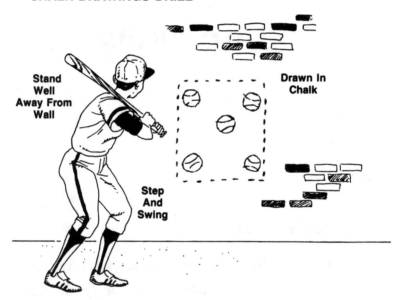

Stand Well Away From Wall

Drawn In Chalk

Step And Swing

HITTING OFF A TEE

Adjustable batting tees are available at most sporting goods stores. A ball is placed on the tee, which can be adjusted to any height. The batter swings and hits the ball off the tee.

When using a tee, attempt to hit the ball squarely. Try not to hit the tee part. It is also best to use a rubber ball or whiffle ball when hitting off a tee.

HITTING OFF BATTING TEE

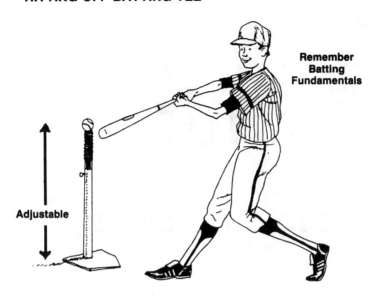

Remember
Batting
Fundamentals

Adjustable

BATTING PRACTICE

The best way to become a better hitter is to hit base-balls—lots of them. This is why batting practice is so important. Get a few friends to go to a ball field. Take turns pitching to each other. Whoever pitches batting practice should remember that the object is to let the batter hit the ball.

The batter should take level swings and just try to meet the ball, timing it right. Never try to "kill the ball" by swinging too hard. You also want to hit the "sweet spot" of the ball with the "sweet spot" of your bat. A "sweet spot" is the place where the best possible ball-bat contact can be made. It varies from batter to batter, so find yours by trying out slightly different swings.

Fielding Drills

PEPPER GAME

"Pepper" is a baseball drill used on all baseball levels, including the pros. It is a batting *and* fielding drill. It can be played with two or more people.

One person is the batter. The others are fielders. The batter faces the fielders. Taking fielding positions, they should stand spread in a line about twenty feet away.

The batter uses a choke grip (see page 24). The batter's job is to practice bat control. One fielder gently pitches the ball to the batter, who lightly taps the ball back to one of the fielders. (Do not take a full swing.) The ball is fielded and thrown back overhand to the batter. The hit-field-throw process is continued.

The batter tries to hit the ball to all of the fielders at different times. Try not to let any pitched balls get past you.

The fielders practice fielding and setting up to throw. After a certain number of hits, another player becomes the batter.

PEPPER GAME

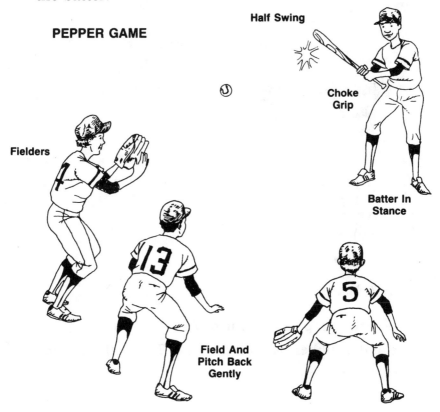

Half Swing

Choke Grip

Fielders

Batter In Stance

Field And Pitch Back Gently

SHAGGING FLIES

"Shagging flies" is a baseball term that means chasing after fly balls. One player is an outfielder (or more than one). A batter tosses the ball up and hits it into the outfield. The ball is caught, thrown in, and then the process is repeated.

SHAGGING FLY BALLS

Crack

OFF A WALL

One of the simplest fielding drills is the best. Get your glove and a rubber ball. Find a wall. Throw the ball off the wall and catch it.

BALL-ROLL DRILL

This is a tiring but excellent ground-ball drill. It takes two players to do it. One player, who's wearing a glove, gets into a fielding position. The other person, who is the roller, faces the fielder. The roller holds a baseball in each hand.

The roller starts the drill by rolling a baseball out to either side of the fielder. The fielder fields the ball and tosses it back to the roller. At the instant the fielder returns the first ball, the roller rolls the ball in the other hand over to the other side of the fielder. The fielder scrambles in the other direction to field the ball. After the ball is fielded and returned, the next ball is rolled again. The roller continues to roll balls.

This drill sounds easy but is extremely tiring. The roller must remember not to roll the balls too far or too fast.

BALL-ROLL DRILL

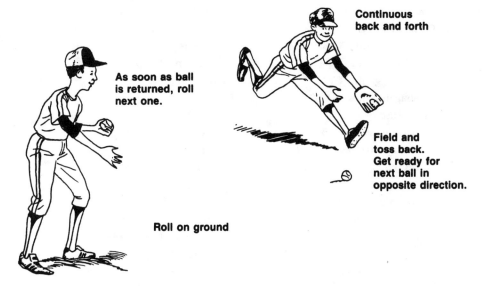

Continuous back and forth

As soon as ball is returned, roll next one.

Field and toss back. Get ready for next ball in opposite direction.

Roll on ground

INDEX